D1172973

This book belongs to

Yareli Rodriguez

Yareli Rodriguez

This edition published by Parragon Books Ltd in 2016
and distributed by

Parragon Inc.
440 Park Avenue South, 13th Floor
New York, NY 10016
www.parragon.com

Copyright © 2016 Disney Enterprises, Inc.

All rights reserved. No part of this publication may be reproduced, stored in a retrieval
system, or transmitted, in any form or by any means, electronic, mechanical, photocopying,
recording, or otherwise, without the prior permission of the copyright holder.

ISBN 978-1-4748-2783-6

Printed in China

Disney
ZOOTOPIA
JUDY'S DREAM FILES

PaRRagon

Bath • New York • Cologne • Melbourne • Delhi
Hong Kong • Shenzhen • Singapore • Amsterdam

Who's Who?

Are you ready to meet some of the creatures living and working in Zootopia? Find out who they are and what they do, then check the circle for your favorite!

Name: Judy Hopps
Species: Rabbit
Prey or Predator: Prey
Job: Police officer, meter maid

Name: Leodore Lionheart
Species: Lion
Prey or Predator: Predator
Job: Mayor of Zootopia

Name: Bellwether
Species: Sheep
Prey or Predator: Prey
Job: Assistant Mayor of Zootopia

Name: Bogo
Species: Cape buffalo
Prey or Predator: Predator
Job: Chief of Police

Name: Clawhauser
Species: Cheetah
Prey or Predator: Predator
Job: Police officer, front desk

Name: Nick Wilde
Species: Fox
Prey or Predator: Predator
Job: Hustler

Name: Finnick
Species: Fennec fox
Prey or Predator: Predator
Job: Hustler

Now that you've met the most important creatures in Zootopia, it's time to tell them all about you! Fill in this fact file.

PASTE IN A PHOTO OR DRAW A PICTURE OF YOURSELF HERE!

Name: yareli

Nickname: yareli / yare

Birthday: November 19 2008

Hair color: Dark Brown

Eye color: Brown

Best friend: Happy

Pets: Dog, Dory, and, Happy

Top talent: pretend play

Worst habit: Handstands

Likes: Shawn mendes
Alexander

Dislikes: Pineapple

Animal Antics

Imagine you are an animal living in Zootopia.... What animal would you be? Circle your top choice from the creatures below, or write an alternate option!

BEAR

Buffalo

Squirrel

LION

Rabbit

ELEPHANT

PANTHER

Mouse

FOX

Sheep

WOLF

RHINO

Cheetah

Shrew

HIPPO Deer

I would be a Rabbit becaus ther cute
like Juty.

Mammal Metropolis

There are lots of different neighborhoods in the bustling city of Zootopia, from Tundratown and Little Rodentia to the Rainforest District. What's it like where you live?

Write the name of the place where you live:

I live in Blue Island

It is a: Town

- ✓ **Town**
- ○ **City**
- ○ **Countryside**

Have you always lived there?

- ✓ **Yes**
- ○ **No**

Check the words that best describe where you live:

- ○ **Busy**
- ✓ **Peaceful**
- ○ **Loud**
- ○ **Friendly**
- ✓ **Quiet**
- ○ **Beautiful**

Where would you like to live in Zootopia?

- ✓ **Bunnyburrow**
- ○ **Tundratown**
- ○ **The Rainforest District**
- ○ **Savannah Central**
- ○ **The Meadowlands**
- ○ **Little Rodentia**

You-topia!

Zootopia is a busy city where all kinds of animals, big and
small, live and work together and anyone can be anything!
If you could build your own city, what would it be like?

Give your city a name:

~~Zootopia~~ puppy paw

Who would live there with you?

My mom, dad, sisters Happy,
Dory, ~~me~~ me, ~~and~~ And brothers.

Check the things your city would have:

- [x] **Movie theater**
- [x] **Restaurants**
- [x] **Playground**
- [ ] **Harbor**
- [x] **Post office**
- [ ] **Sports stadium**
- [x] **Shopping mall**
- [x] **Bank**
- [ ] **Wildlife park**
- [x] **Beach**

The Zootopia motto is "Anyone can be anything!"
Give your city its own motto:

....

....

DRAW A PICTURE OF YOUR CITY HERE.
DON'T FORGET TO INCLUDE YOUR HOUSE!

Home Sweet Home!

When Judy Hopps moves out of her family home in Bunnyburrow, she lives in an apartment in downtown Zootopia. She has two very noisy neighbors, Kudu and Oryx! Tell Judy all about your home....

Do you have neighbors?

[✓] **Yes**   [ ] **No**

Do you have your own room or do you share?

[✓] **Own room**   [✓] **Shared room**

Describe your home:

....
....
....

Describe your bedroom:

....
....
....

What's your favorite part of your home?

....
....

PASTE IN A PHOTO OR DRAW A PICTURE OF YOUR HOME HERE!

Family Files

Judy has a large family, with lots of bunny cousins! She misses them when she moves away from Bunnyburrow, but they keep in touch by video chat. Judy would love to learn a bit about your family....

Mom's name: Monica

Dad's name: Eric

Brothers' names: Micel, Junior, Alejundro, Damion.

Sisters' names: Yohanni, Cindy, Me.

PASTE IN A PHOTO OF YOUR FAMILY.

Who makes you laugh the most?

Dad

Who is the best at helping out?

Dad Mom

Who is the noisiest?

Mom

Who gives the best hugs?

sister

Check the words you think best describe your family:

- ( ) Large
- (✓) Noisy
- (✓) Fun
- (✓) Smart
- (✓) Happy
- (✓) Small
- (✓) Talented
- (✓) Helpful

JUDY'S PARENTS, STU AND BONNIE, ARE SO PROUD OF HER.

Dream BIG!

Judy dreams of being a cop, keeping creatures safe, and making Zootopia a better place. What are your biggest dreams? Check your answers in the lists below.

My dream job:
- ☆ Astronaut
- ✓ Police officer
- ☆ Pirate
- ☆ Artist
- ☆ Explorer
- ☆ Dancer

My dream vacation:
- ✓ Beach
- ☆ Rainforest
- ☆ Desert
- ☆ Mountain
- ☆ Jungle
- ☆ City

My dream animal:
- ☆ Lion
- ☆ Squirrel
- ☆ Monkey
- ☆ Polar bear
- ☆ Giraffe
- ✓ Rabbit

My dream home:
- ☆ Castle
- ☆ Igloo
- ☆ Submarine
- ☆ Tepee
- ☆ Mansion
- ☆ Cave

THE ZOOTOPIA MOTTO:
"Anyone can be anything!"

WRITE ABOUT YOUR DREAMS FOR THE FUTURE!

I want to be a petStore
Owner.

Judy and Nick are very different creatures, but that doesn't stop them becoming best friends. Fill in everything you know about your best friends!

Friends Fur-ever!

Friend 1

Name: Zuri

Birthday: ....

What I like best about them: fun
Funny

Something we have in common: We like
playing a lot.

Something that makes us different:
She is littrel I'm big.

Paste in a picture!

Friend 2

Name: Angel

Birthday: 2009

What I like best about them:
....

Something we have in common:
....

Something that makes us different:
boy girl

Paste in a picture!

Friend 3 Cindy

Name: ....

Birthday: ....

What I like best about them: She So
Nice I like her.........................

Something we have in common:

....

Something that makes us different: She is
Older. I am Smaller

Friend 4

Name: Alexa ....

Birthday: ....

What I like best about them:

....

Something we have in common:

....

Something that makes us different:

....

Friend 5 Alexander

Name: ....

Birthday: ....

What I like best about them:

....

Something we have in common:

....

Something that makes us different:

....

Paste in a picture!

Paste in a picture!

Paste in a picture!

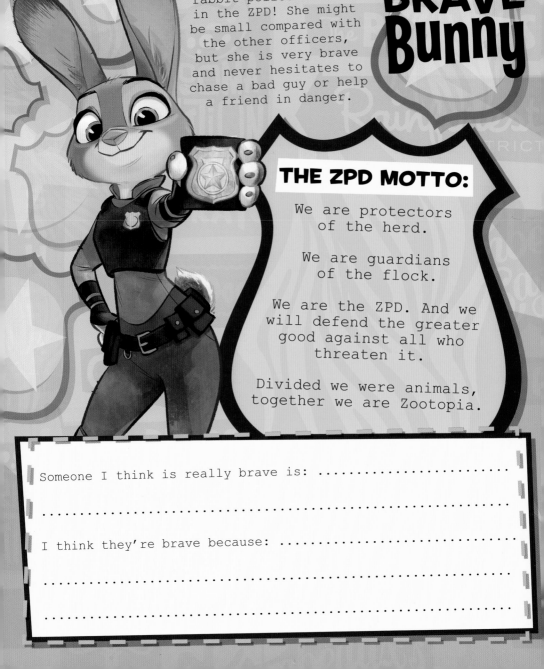

Judy is the first rabbit police officer in the ZPD! She might be small compared with the other officers, but she is very brave and never hesitates to chase a bad guy or help a friend in danger.

BRAVE Bunny

THE ZPD MOTTO:

We are protectors of the herd.

We are guardians of the flock.

We are the ZPD. And we will defend the greater good against all who threaten it.

Divided we were animals, together we are Zootopia.

Someone I think is really brave is: ....

....

I think they're brave because: ....

....

....

Think of a time when you were brave and write all
about it here. Then the next time you feel scared,
you can look back at what you've written
and remember how brave you really are!

A time when I was really brave was:

. . . .

. . . .

. . . .

. . . .

. . . .

. . . .

. . . .

. . . .

. . . .

. . . .

. . . .

. . . .

. . . .

Dream Team

Judy loves being a cop and feeling like she's part of a team. It's even better when Nick joins the ZPD and she has a partner! Imagine your dream team.... You could play a sport, dance on stage, be superheroes, or even fight crime!

What would your team be called?

Team ....

How many members would it have? ....

Who would be part of your team?

Write their names here and give them each a special team nickname!

TEAM MEMBER 1

Name: ...Alexander.....

Nickname: ...Alex........

TEAM MEMBER 2

Name: ...Alexa.........

Nickname: ...Rosie......

TEAM MEMBER 3

Name: ...Cindy.........

Nickname: ...Rosie......

TEAM MEMBER 4

Name: ...me yareli.....

Nickname: ...lenet......

DESIGN AND COLOR A COOL UNIFORM FOR YOUR TEAM HERE!

Nick is wily and cunning. Judy is brave and kind. Look at all the words listed below and choose the best one to describe each of your friends!

Which Word?

Happy

SMART

Brave

Funny

SHY

KIND

Serious

Musical

COOL

Stylish

Imaginative

CONFIDENT

Silly

Caring

GENEROUS

Friend 1

Name: ....

Word: ....

Friend 2

Name: ....

Word: ....

Friend 3

Name: ....

Word: ....

Friend 4

Name: ....

Word: ....

Friend 5

Name: ....

Word: ....

What word would your friends pick to describe you?

Word: ....

Opposites Attract!

Nick and Judy are opposites in lots of ways, but despite their differences they become friends and stick together through thick and thin.

Judy

- FEMALE
- LITTLE
- PREY
- COP
- GOOD

Nick

- MALE
- BIG
- PREDATOR
- HUSTLER
- NAUGHTY

Hot **Cold**

Circle which you prefer from these pairs of opposites.

Sweet *Sour*

Summer Winter

Tall Short

Indoors Outdoors

Wet **Dry**

Sunny Cloudy

Smooth Rough

Light **Dark**

Early Late

Day Night

Predator Prey

Hard **Soft**

Full Empty

Loud Quiet

Black White

A Helping Hand

Together Nick and Judy are a dynamic crime-fighting, mystery-solving duo. They are always there to help each other out! Which of your friends or family would you choose to help you in the following situations?

You can't answer a question in your homework.

I would ask ....DaD.................................... for help.

You've forgotten the lyrics to a song.

I would ask ...MY...Sister........................... for help.

You need to pick an outfit for a special event.

I would ask ....DaD................................... for help.

You want to create a new dance routine.

I would ask .... for help.

You're stuck on a level of a computer game.

I would ask ....eNYONe........................ for help.

You need to plan a surprise party.

I would ask ....DaD...MOM..................... for help.

Nick helped Judy to solve a huge crime
and save Zootopia! Write about a time when
a friend helped you to solve a problem.

....

....

....

....

....

....

....

....

....

....

....

....

....

....

Prey or PRED?

In Zootopia, prey and predators live together in harmony ... most of the time! Which would you be? Take the test to find out!

1) You hear a strange noise during the night. Do you ...

 a. Go investigate   **b. Hide under the covers**

2) What is your favorite kind of sport?

 a. Solo sport   **b. Team sport**

3) What do you do when you feel angry?

 a. Shout and scream!   **b. Go for a long walk**

4) How would you describe your sense of style?

 a. I stand out from the crowd!   **b. I like to fit in**

5) In your spare time you like to ...

 a. Have me-time   ✓ **b. Hang out with friends**

6) Your favorite food is ...

 a. A juicy burger   **b. A nice fresh salad**

MOSTLY As:
You're a predator!

You have a big
personality and
a hot temper.
You always stand
out from the crowd!

MOSTLY Bs:
You're a prey animal!

You're a little bit
shy but love hanging
out with a big group
of close friends!

REMEMBER, WHETHER YOU'RE PREY OR PRED, YOU CAN BE ANYTHING YOU WANT TO BE!

Well Done!

Being the first rabbit police officer in the ZPD is a big achievement for Judy. Use these pages to write about some of your biggest achievements!

Something I did for the first time ...

Date: 05-01-16

What I did: Handstand

How I felt: Happy

Somewhere I went for the first time ...

Date: 06-17+17 Nobel

Where I went: Books And nobel

How I felt: exided

Somebody I helped ...

Date:...

What I did: ....

....

How I felt: ....

Something I was proud of ...

Date:...

What I did: ....

....

How I felt: ....

My biggest achievement ...

Date:...

What I did: ....

....

How I felt: ....

Animal PALS

While they try to solve the big case together, Judy and Nick make all sorts of new friends. Write about your own animal friends here!

IF YOU DON'T HAVE ANY ANIMAL FRIENDS, MAKE SOME UP! LET YOUR IMAGINATION RUN WILD!

Animal pal 1

Name: Happy

Type of animal: Puppy

Color: white

Favorite food: everything

Draw or paste in a picture!

Animal pal 2

Name: bella

Type of animal: puppy

Color: black and peachy brown

Favorite food: chicen

Draw or paste in a picture!

Animal pal 3

Name: ...Dory.................................

Type of animal: ...Fat Dog...................

Color: ...brown black white.................

Favorite food: ...Dog Food...............

Draw or paste in a picture!

Animal pal 4

Name: ....

Type of animal: ....

Color: ....

Favorite food: ....

Draw or paste in a picture!

Animal pal 5

Name: ....

Type of animal: ....

Color: ....

Favorite food: ....

Draw or paste in a picture!

Hero Files

HERO of Zootopia

Judy Hopps

This person is a hero because:

She makes Zootopia a better place, helps her friends, and proves that anyone really can be anything!

Number 1 HERO

Paste in a picture!

Name:

. . . .

This person is a hero because:

. . . .

. . . .

HERO at home

Paste in a picture!

Name:

. . . .

This person is a hero because:

. . . .

. . . .

HERO from the movies

Paste in a picture!

Name:

. . . .

This person is a hero because:

. . . .

. . . .

HERO at school

Paste in a picture!

Name:

. . . .

This person is a hero because:

. . . .

. . . .

All the animals of Zootopia have a favorite food. Finnick loves Jumbo-pops, Clawhauser the cheetah loves doughnuts, and Judy loves carrots! Tell them about YOUR favorite foods.

Favorite Foods

My favorite breakfast is:

Pan kacs

My favorite lunch is:

Makatony

My favorite dinner is:

grill meat

My favorite snack is:

hot cheeps

Check your favorite tastes from the list below:

- ( ) Sweet
- (✓) Sour
- ( ) Tangy
- ( ) Savory
- ( ) Salty
- (✓) Spicy

DRAW OR PASTE IN A PICTURE OF YOUR PERFECT MEAL. IT CAN BE ANYTHING YOU WANT!

Mick Donend.

chikenugets hisy
O O O O

Bufelow